To Matthew
Happy 9# Birthday!
Love
Uncle
&
Aunty Pauline
X X o o

The Great Tooth Fairy Rip-Off

Dori Hillestad Butler

illustrated by Jack Lindstrom

Fairview Press
Minneapolis

Library of Congress Cataloging-in-Publication Data

Butler, Dori Hillestad.
  The great Tooth Fairy rip-off / Dori Hillestad Butler : illustrated by Jack Lindstrom.
        p.   cm.
  Summary: Joey tries to negotiate with the Tooth Fairy for the amount he thinks his tooth is really worth, but he gets a surprise and learns the values of work, money, and saving when the Tooth Fairy starts bargaining back.
  ISBN 1-57749-023-1
  [1. Tooth Fairy—Fiction. 2. Money—Fiction.] I. Lindstrom, Jack, ill. II. Title.
  PZ7.B9759Gr   1997
  [E]—dc20   96-38687
                                                                              CIP
                                                                              AC

Edited by Robyn Hansen
Cover design by Circus Design

First Printing: February 1997
Printed in the United States of America

01 00 99 98 97   7 6 5 4 3 2 1

Published by Fairview Press, 2450 Riverside Avenue South, Minneapolis, MN 55454.

For a current catalog of Fairview Press titles, please call this toll-free number: 1-800-544-8207

Publisher's Note: Fairview Press publishes books and other materials related to the subjects of family and social issues. Its publications, including *The Great Tooth Fairy Rip-Off*, do not necessarily reflect the philosophy of Fairview Hospital and Healthcare Services or their treatment programs.

The paper used in this publication meets the minimum requirements of American National Standard for Information Sciences—Permanence of Paper for Printed Library Materials, ANSI Z329.48-1984.

For Bob, who not only believed in me,
but taught me to believe in myself

Joey's bottom front tooth was loose. He liked to press his tongue against the tooth and wiggle it back and forth. Joey was wiggling his tooth during a kickball game when suddenly the tooth popped out.

"Hey!" Joey cried, holding up his tooth for everyone to see. "I lost my first tooth!"

The game stopped and Joey's friends crowded around him.

"You'll have to put your tooth under your pillow," said Alex.

"Yeah, then the tooth fairy will give you a quarter," added Missy.

"A quarter!" Brandon sneered. "She gave *me* a whole dollar!"

"Really?" asked Joey. He'd been trying to save up a dollar so he could buy a pack of dinosaur stickers.

That night Joey scrubbed his tooth really good. He was pretty sure he'd get a dollar for it. But maybe if it was extra clean, he'd get two dollars.

He carefully wrapped his tooth in a tissue and set it under his pillow. Then he went to sleep.

The next morning, he felt under his pillow. The tissue was gone. And in its place Joey found one, two, three, four coins. One quarter. One nickel. And two dimes.

Joey groaned. One quarter, one nickel, and two dimes was not a dollar. It was only fifty cents.

Maybe the other fifty cents fell off his bed during the night. Joey leaned over and checked under his bed. But all he saw under there was a few stuffed animals, some games, and some dirty clothes.

He checked between the sheets, inside his pillowcase, even in the pocket on his pajamas. But there were no other coins. Fifty cents was all he got.

Later that morning, he went to the Park Street Store with Brandon and his dad. Brandon's dad gave Brandon money to buy the dinosaur stickers. But since Joey didn't have enough for the stickers, he bought a candy bar instead.

"It's not fair," Joey grumbled, munching on his candy bar. "I should've gotten more than fifty cents for my tooth."

Brandon agreed. "If I were you, I'd write a letter to the tooth fairy and tell her she has to give you more money or she can't keep the tooth. Fifty cents is a rip-off!"

So Joey went home and wrote
a letter to the tooth fairy.

That looked good. Joey put the note under his pillow when he went to bed.

The next morning he found a note from the tooth fairy. His tooth was taped to the bottom.

Joey didn't think the tooth fairy would return his tooth. He certainly didn't think she'd ask for her fifty cents back. Now what was he supposed to do? He'd already spent the fifty cents.

"I'll pay you fifty cents to clean your room," his mom offered.

So Joey cleaned his room. First he picked up everything on the floor. Then he cleaned under his bed. He even cleaned his closet. He dusted and vacuumed. When he was finished, he called his mom.

"Your room looks very nice, Joey," she said, handing him two shiny quarters.

Joey put the quarters under his pillow. Then he sat on his bed and stared at his tooth. What was he going to do with an old baby tooth?

If I was the tooth fairy, I'd plant it and wave my wand and make it grow into a flower, Joey thought.

Or maybe I'd turn it in to the head tooth fairy at Toothfairyland so she could use it to build a new road or a new house.

Maybe the head tooth fairy would think it was such a good tooth she'd give me a vacation to Disneyland.

Joey sighed. He wasn't the tooth fairy. And he'd much rather have fifty cents than an old tooth.

He wondered whether the tooth fairy would be willing to take his tooth back and let him keep the fifty cents he earned cleaning his room. There was one way to find out.

Joey wrapped his tooth in another tissue and set it under his pillow beside the two shiny quarters. Then he wrote another note.

The next morning, Joey peeked under his pillow. The tooth was gone and the two shiny quarters were still there.

Joey took the coins to his dinosaur bank and dropped them in. He only needed another fifty cents to buy the dinosaur stickers he wanted. Maybe he could do some more work around the house to earn it.

But before Joey went to ask his mom about that, he opened his mouth and checked for other loose teeth.

My name is *Matthew* _____

_____.

I am _____ years old.

The day I lost my first tooth was _____

_____.

The Tooth Fairy brought me _____

_____.

Other children's books from Fairview Press

Alligator in the Basement, by Bob Keeshan, TV's Captain Kangaroo
illustrated by Kyle Corkum

Box-Head Boy, by Christine M. Winn with David Walsh, Ph.D.
illustrated by Christine M. Winn

Clover's Secret, by Christine M. Winn with David Walsh, Ph.D.
illustrated by Christine M. Winn

Hurry, Murray, Hurry!, by Bob Keeshan, TV's Captain Kangaroo
illustrated by Chad Peterson

I'll Go to School If . . . , by Bo Flood
illustrated by Ronnie Walter Shipman

Monster Boy, by Christine M. Winn with David Walsh, Ph.D.
illustrated by Christine M. Winn

My Dad Has HIV, by Earl Alexander, Sheila Rudin, Pam Sejkora
illustrated by Ronnie Walter Shipman

The Story Dance, by Barbara Satterfield
illustrated by Fran Gregory

"Wonderful You" Series, by Slim Goodbody
illustrated by Terry Boles
The Body
The Mind
The Spirit